P9-DWB-507

ANYTHING CAN HAPPEN,
YOU JUST HAVE TO BELIEVE!

Minerva Mint

capstone
young readers

Minerva Mint is published by Capstone Young Readers
A Capstone Imprint
1710 Roe Crest Drive
North Mankato, Minnesota 56003
www.capstoneyoungreaders.com

Text by Elisa Puricelli Guerra; Translated by Chris Turner
Original edition published by Edizioni Piemme S.p.A., Italy
Original title: La compagnia delle civette

International Rights © Atlantyca S.p.A., via Leopardi 8 - 20123 Milano – Italia —
foreignrights@atlantyca.it — www.atlantyca.com

Library of Congress Cataloging-in-Publication Data is available
on the Library of Congress website.

ISBN: 978-1-62370-038-6 (hardcover)
ISBN: 978-1-4342-6510-4 (library binding)
ISBN: 978-1-4342-6513-5 (paperback)

Summary:
When a couple comes to Minerva's mansion claiming to be her parents, she knows
they are lying. She just has to prove it.

Designer:
Veronica Scott

Printed in China by Nordica.
1013/CA21301908
092013   007736NORDS14

THE ORDER
OF
THE OWLS

by Elisa Puricelli Guerra

illustrated by Gabo León Bernstein

TABLE OF CONTENTS

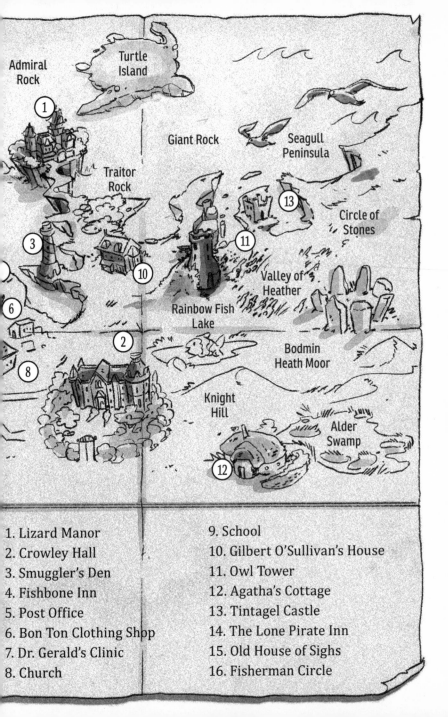

1. Lizard Manor
2. Crowley Hall
3. Smuggler's Den
4. Fishbone Inn
5. Post Office
6. Bon Ton Clothing Shop
7. Dr. Gerald's Clinic
8. Church
9. School
10. Gilbert O'Sullivan's House
11. Owl Tower
12. Agatha's Cottage
13. Tintagel Castle
14. The Lone Pirate Inn
15. Old House of Sighs
16. Fisherman Circle

EVENING NEWS

BABY FOUND IN BAG AT VICTORIA STATION

March 22nd, London – This morning a baby girl, just a few months old, was found in a travel bag in a waiting room at Victoria Station.

The bag was made of leather and, allegedly, rather fancy, with the initials "MM" engraved on its brass buckle. It seemed well used and was covered with stickers from all kinds of exotic places: Egypt, Beijing, Timbuktu, Tahiti, and even the Dark Jungle.

In addition to the little girl, the bag contained a book (*The Universal Encyclopedia, Vol. IV, M–P*), an envelope addressed to Mr. Septimus Hodge of Torrington Place, London, and the deed to a house called "Lizard Manor" at 1 Admiral Rock, Cornwall.

In all my years as a reporter, I've never seen anything like it! The girl's parents must be very forgetful to have left her in the waiting room of a London railway station.

Fortunately, she was found by a station custodian, Geraldine Flopps. Mrs. Flopps told reporters, "I was mopping the waiting room floor when I found something under a bench; it was the baby. She was in a travel bag."

Flopps took the baby to the lost property office, where they'd never seen anything like it. "People lose all kinds of weird stuff, but a baby?!" said Mr. Carson, the manager. Carson called the station master, who called the station manager, who called the head of the railways, who called a lawyer and a social services officer.

No one knew what to do. According to the rules,

anything found in the station becomes the property of the railways until the owner comes to collect it. They all agreed, though, that a baby couldn't possibly be left in a lost property office until her forgetful parents came back.

Flopps explained that the people in the lost property office — who'd more or less ignored her during the whole conversation — all suddenly started staring at her. "Would you like to look after the baby?" asked the social services officer with a hopeful expression.

Flopps explained that she lives in a studio apartment in Talgarth Road, West London. It's an area that's full of traffic, noise, smog, and smelly fish-and-chip shops. She told them that her apartment wasn't at all well suited for a baby.

The lawyer reportedly pretended not to hear as he examined the deed to the house. "It's a pity that we cannot read the owner's name," he was reported as saying. "But it's all perfectly legal. The baby and Mrs. Flopps shall live at Lizard Manor until the parents come to claim them. The house and the child, obviously, not Mrs. Flopps." Geraldine Flopps had no chance to say anything before the lawyer added, "But first, the baby needs a name."

During a lengthy discussion among the station master, the station manager, the head of the railways, and the lawyer (the social services officer had left by this stage to look after some other case), Flopps spotted a bird perched on a sign in front of one of the many stores in the station. It was a huge snowy owl, a bird rarely found in London train stations. The sign read: Minerva Beauty — Five Pound Perms!

"How about Minerva?" Flopps asked. She then looked around in search of inspiration for a surname. She even checked her pockets, where she found a squashed peppermint candy. "Minerva Mint?"

The lawyer breathed a reported sigh of relief. "Well, it's all decided, then,"

he said, writing the name on the deed. "Minerva Mint." He then solemnly handed the bag and its contents to Mrs. Flopps.

Tomorrow, Flopps will leave her old life in London behind her for her new home in Cornwall.

I would like to make an appeal to the forgetful parents: Come and collect your child! She's waiting for you at Lizard Manor, 1 Admiral Rock, Cornwall.

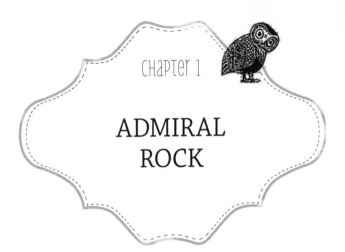

CHAPTER 1

ADMIRAL
ROCK

Two bare feet stuck out from under an orange tent in the middle of a bedroom. The toes scrunched and unscrunched in time with a gentle snoring. There were other sounds, too: the howling of the wind and the constant *plip-plop* of the rain as it leaked down onto everything in the room, including a big, uncomfortable looking bed. If you listened hard, you could also hear a quiet *nibble-nibble*. The mice were already awake.

A clock, which until that moment had been ticking

away calmly on the bedside table, suddenly let out an alarming clatter. The bare feet immediately disappeared into the tent, replaced a second later by a big, yawning mouth. Minerva, who was wearing blue pajamas at least two sizes too big for her, shot out of the tent to turn off the alarm.

She looked around and smiled. It wasn't the leaky room that made her smile. And it wasn't the dark, stormy day she could see out the window. Minerva was smiling because it was March 22nd, her ninth birthday. And it was going to be a very busy day!

Well, March 22nd wasn't exactly Minerva's birthday, but it was exactly nine years ago today that Mrs. Flopps had found her in the travel bag at Victoria Station. And there was something that Minerva did every March 22nd as soon as she woke up.

First she took a deep breath and stuck out her chest as if she was about to dive into a swimming pool. Then she stuck her head under the big bed with its brass headboard, reached through the dust balls, grabbed a travel bag, and pulled it out with a huge sneeze. She dragged the bag back into the tent.

She ran her finger over the initials engraved on the buckle and opened it with a click. She felt that familiar empty feeling in her tummy. Inside the bag were things of high importance. First there was a light blue folder where she kept all the newspaper articles about Mrs. Flopps finding her in the waiting room. There were at least a dozen of them, and they made her feel like a celebrity. She'd read them all hundreds of times.

What she found much more interesting, though, was the big book with its red cover and title in golden letters: *The Universal Encyclopedia, Vol. IV, M–P.* Minerva had read all one hundred fifty pages of it, always wondering why that particular book should have been in her bag. Why M through P? She'd thought about that a lot, and in the end, decided that her parents had put it in the bag because the words *mama* and *papa* were under the letters *M* and *P*.

Page 25 read, "A mama gives you unconditional love."

Page 107 read, "A papa will always protect you."

And Minerva always felt both loved and protected every time she looked through the huge book.

But there had to be something else in that book. She was sure of it. Something that she'd missed. Something that might help her find her parents. She just had to look more carefully.

Minerva laid the book on her lap and reached for the oil lamp she used to light up the tent. But the moment she began reading, a loud screeching made her jump. She snapped the book shut, put it on the floor, and ran out of the tent and over to the window.

The storm was raging in the garden. Rain was lashing everything. The wind was blowing the trees as if it was angry with them and wanted to uproot them all. Minerva cupped her hands against the glass and looked out. In the distance, she could see someone coming up the cliff. She blinked twice and muttered, "Who could that be?"

She hurtled out of the room, into the dark, cold upstairs hallway, and down the stairs. The steps creaked as if they wanted to say hello to the new arrival as well.

* * *

Ravi Kapoor rode along the top of Admiral Rock, struggling against the wind and rain as it tried to pull him off his bike. His brakes made a terrible screech every time he slowed down to avoid a pothole. In front of him, perched on the cliff top like a figure-head on a ship, was Lizard Manor. It eyed him grimly through its empty windows.

Ravi had only just moved to Cornwall, but he'd already heard lots of terrible stories about Lizard Manor, including that it was haunted. It had stood empty for so many years that no one in the village could even remember who the last owners had been. He'd also heard that the current owners were . . . really, really weird.

Ravi was so distracted by all these thoughts that

he almost ran into another pothole. He swerved to miss it and just about flew off the cliff. He stopped for a moment to calm down and check that the box was still attached to his bike rack. He then rode off again, without once looking at the sea on his left. Everyone knew that Ravi was afraid of heights, but his mom had sent him up there just the same!

He could hardly wait to leave the box by the door and get away. But the moment he finally stopped in front of the house — with another earsplitting screech of brakes — the big door swung open. There was a girl standing there. She was wearing pajamas that were too big for her and a blue nightcap with a mass of red, curly hair sticking out from under it. Two big green eyes peered at him from amid a sea of freckles.

"Um . . . hi," Ravi greeted her. "I've got something to deliver."

"I know," answered Minerva. "I've been expecting you."

The day before, she'd gone to the general store

in Pembrose, the nearest village. The store was also the post office and the only place to buy groceries. Minerva had met Mrs. Kapoor. With her gentle, sing-song voice, the woman had told her about the long journey that she and her son, Ravi, had just made to get from Mumbai, India, to Cornwall.

Minerva couldn't be happier about Ravi and his mom buying the general store. Mrs. Kapoor played happy music and burned incense. And instead of the old, stale crackers that the previous owners left out, she offered bowls of exotic fruit to her customers. Ravi's mother had bronze skin, shimmering black hair, and a red dot in the middle of her forehead. And she always wore a sari, a traditional Indian dress.

Minerva looked Ravi up and down and eventually decided that he had friend potential. The previous deliveryman had been elderly and would always arrive at the front door huffing and puffing like a steam engine. He was as deaf as a post, too, and no good for chatting with. This boy, though . . .

She'd watched him ride up the cliff like a champion cyclist!

Ravi was actually running late for school. So he jumped off his bike, grabbed the box of groceries, and handed it to Minerva. "This is —" But just then, something big and heavy fell on his head. "Oww!" he yelled, dropping the box. He started jumping all around, waving his arms about to get the thing off of him.

Minerva tried to calm him down. "Hey, stop jumping about! It's only Augustus! You'll frighten him!"

"Who?" Ravi stopped jumping up and down and looked up.

Obligingly, Augustus flew down onto Ravi's shoulder. Ravi carefully turned his head and found himself face to face with a big white owl. The bird stared at him with its round eyes, as yellow as fire. It then tilted its big feathery head and began to move jerkily, as if it was dancing to music that only it could hear. It finally rolled its eyes and cried, "*Woot! Woot!*"

Minerva reached out her hand to pet Augustus.

"He's a snowy owl," she explained. "He's here to say goodnight before going to sleep." She pointed to the roof. "He's made his nest in one of the chimneys with all the other owls."

"Th-there are others?" Ravi stammered, without taking his eyes off Augustus. He knew nothing about owls. Even less about snowy ones.

"There are fourteen all together!" answered Minerva. Augustus made a loud *Woot! Woot!* as if he was agreeing with her. He then spread his wings and, majestically and silently, flew up to the roof.

"Wow!" exclaimed Ravi.

"Don't you have owls in Mumbai?" Minerva asked, pulling up her nightcap, which had fallen down over her face.

"I don't know . . ." answered Ravi, still with one eye on the roof. "At least, I've never seen one."

"They're good luck, you know."

Minerva suddenly remembered something. "Yikes! I've gotta go!" she exclaimed. "The foxes are still locked in the living room!" She rushed back inside. Then, as if she'd just remembered something else, she stopped and turned to Ravi, who was about to get back onto his bike. "Hang on!" she cried. "Do you want to come to my birthday party this afternoon?"

Ravi felt cornered. If he didn't say yes, he'd sound rude. But the last thing he wanted to do was ride all the way back up the cliff again. "Okay," he finally said with a sigh.

Minerva's face brightened. "Cool! See you at four! Bring someone with you, if you like."

Ravi hesitated, but he decided the ride would be better if he came back with another person. "I could ask Thomasina Crowley. She's in my grade."

Minerva gave him a big smile. "Great!" she exclaimed. She was about to go inside again. Then, suddenly, she rushed over to Ravi and started shaking his hand so hard that she almost knocked him off his bike. "I'm so silly!" she cried. "My name's Minerva Mint! I already know yours. It's Ravi!"

He took his aching hand back — Minerva had a great grip! "Um . . . yeah . . . I'm very pleased to meet you," he said, like his mother had taught him. "Okay, I'll see you later then." He pedaled off back down the hill, his brakes screeching loudly every few seconds.

Minerva picked up the box of groceries and went back inside, feeling very happy. It wasn't even eight in the morning, but so many things had already happened! She had a new friend. And she was about to meet Thomasina Crowley. All she knew about Thomasina was that she lived at Crowley Hall. Her home was a magnificent mansion where every-thing — from the lawn to the lace curtains — was always neat and tidy. The exact opposite of Lizard Manor!

CHapTer 2

BEWARE OF THE FOXES

Minerva took the groceries into kitchen number two. They hadn't used kitchen number one since a pipe burst and it had flooded. All things considered, Minerva thought she was lucky. Not everyone could say they lived in a house with more than fifty rooms, not including the attic and basement.

There were three kitchens (really handy if one flooded), thirty-one bedrooms (one for each day of the month), nine bathrooms (so you never had to wait if you needed to go), five lounge rooms (although one was full of foxes), a huge library (although you did have to be careful opening the old books since they were ready to fall apart). And then there were three more rooms that she hadn't even found yet. Minerva was sure that there was at least one secret passage somewhere, too, but she hadn't found that yet, either.

She sometimes felt a little alone in that big house, but there were always lots of things to do. Like fixing the big cast-iron stove in kitchen number two. It actually made so much smoke that Minerva couldn't even see where she was going. Thinking she was putting the box on the table, she dropped it on the floor with a huge thump.

The thump was answered by a whole lot more thumps. They weren't echoes, which were quite normal in a house that size. Someone was knocking furiously at the front door.

Minerva sped back off down the hallway. Her nightcap, which was as big for her as her pajamas, fell right down over her face. She flung the door open and found herself staring at a pair of smartly dressed people, who were obviously from London. The man was wearing a suit and tie and had an umbrella under one arm. The woman had high heels and a thin silk scarf tied around her long neck. A fire-engine-red car was parked in the driveway.

Both of them seemed surprised. They'd rung the bell again and again, but no one had come. Then they'd tried knocking and suddenly this small person whose whole head was covered by a nightcap appeared.

The woman was the first to talk. "We are Mr. and Mrs. Greatbore," she chirped. "We would like to see Mrs. Flopps, please. We rang the doorbell repeatedly but no one opened."

"Of course not! It's broken!" said Minerva, eyeing the couple through her frayed nightcap.

"Oh, I see. Are we addressing Mrs. Flopps?"

"Oh, no! She's in the garden painting."

"In this weather?!" said the man in surprise. He had a perfectly groomed mustache that was thin and wiry.

"Mrs. Flopps paints in any weather," answered Minerva, pulling a face as if she'd just smelled something bad. She'd actually just figured out who those people were.

Every year, two days before Minerva's birthday,

Mrs. Flopps put on her best suit and hat. Then she strode down to the general store to put an announcement in the *Times*, the most important newspaper in Britain.

It was always the same:

Would the parents of Minerva Mint, the owners of a huge mansion with ocean views, please contact Mrs. Geraldine Flopps, Lizard Manor, 1 Admiral Rock, Cornwall?

Each year a couple of imposters would answer, thinking that a huge mansion with ocean views sounded quite delightful. The house was in urgent need of repair, but it was on such a big piece of land that it was probably the most wonderful place in all the British Isles.

Minerva had a sixth sense for spotting phonies. And these two had "phony" written all over their faces. She pulled her nightcap back, revealing her inquisitive green eyes.

"Oh, you must be Minerva!" exclaimed Mrs. Greatbore, her eyelashes fluttering. Then, to Minerva's enormous horror, she tried to hug her. "My little one! After all this time!" She nodded at her husband. "Arthur, this is our dear child! Isn't this wonderful!"

Then suddenly both of them tried to hug her.

Minerva cleverly gave them the slip and then did something that left them both speechless. First she hopped on her right foot three times and then three times on her left. Her face turned as red as if she'd just eaten a chili, and her eyes even started watering. "I'm . . . I'm very happy to meet you!" she said with a sob.

"Don't cry, honey!" exclaimed Mrs. Greatbore. "We're all together again, and we love you so much! Arthur, say something!"

"Um . . . there, there," muttered Arthur, giving Minerva a pat on the shoulder. "We're . . . ahem . . . all together again."

Minerva was anything but touched by the reunion. She was doing her very best not to burst out laughing. "Would you like to see the house?" she asked. "Sorry, but there's water dripping everywhere.

There are great big holes in the roof, you know. We're just lucky that the whole thing doesn't fall down on top of us."

They went into the huge, dark hallway, where the only light came from outside. On the left was a suit of armor, although it was missing a leg and an arm. Horrible stuffed animal heads hung all over the walls, with their shiny glass eyes peering at their every move.

They then followed another shadowy corridor with several doors on both sides. The Greatbores looked all around them with greedy expressions. "How many rooms are there, my little one?" asked Daphne Greatbore.

"Fifty-five," answered Minerva. "Not counting the attic and basement." The Greatbores exchanged a look.

Meanwhile, thick black smoke continued to pour out from kitchen number two. The old wooden floor creaked in protest under their every step: *eeek, eeek, eeek!* Long, silky cobwebs hung from the ceiling, moving gracefully in the drafty house. Spiders were welcome guests at Lizard Manor. And they came in all shapes and sizes.

"Is this the living room?" asked Daphne. Without waiting for an answer, she opened a door. The second she did, a huge fox knocked her clean off her feet. The beautiful, tawny animal was immediately followed by four little foxes and then another big one.

"Oops! I forgot to get them out!" exclaimed Minerva. The visitors had distracted her.

"Arthur!" cried Mrs. Greatbore, as she grabbed onto her husband to drag herself up. "We're being attacked by foxes!"

Minerva was about to say that it was only Ginger, Cinnamon, and their babies, and that they lived in living room number three because the sofa was so comfy. But . . . perhaps this was the chance she was waiting for.

As loudly as she could, Minerva screamed out, "Look out! They're wild foxes! They're really, really dangerous!"

"Arthur!" Daphne cried. "Get me out of here! Foxes have rabies!"

Arthur hoisted up his wife under her arms and led her back to the front door, waving his umbrella wildly in front of him to ward off any fox attacks.

Once they'd made it outside, Daphne, who was as pale as a ghost, recovered a little. "I feel much be—" she began, but the words died on her lips. She put her hands over her head and screamed, "Arthur! They're attacking us from the sky!"

Minerva looked up. Two huge snowy owls were swooping down toward them. And they really were terrifying: as silent and solemn as ghosts.

Arthur started waving his umbrella in the air to protect his wife. But the owls, who thought this strange human was just playing a game, started swooping all around them faster and faster.

"*Woot! Woot!*"

"*Woot! Woot!*"

"Run to the car, Daphne!" Arthur cried, waving his umbrella around and trying to shield his

wife with his body. He pushed her through the driver's door and scrambled in behind her. He started the engine, just as even more owls were coming to join in the fun.

Now that she was safely in the car, Daphne began to breathe more easily. She wound down the window (just a little) and called out to Minerva, "Darling, we've written to a lawyer at the Department of Child Welfare. They'll be here in a week to decide whether you can come and live with us. In the meantime, we should get to know each other better." She paused. "Um . . . can you recommend a good hotel near here? We don't want to disturb Mrs. Flopps. . . . We'll be back later when she's . . . um . . . finished painting."

Minerva frowned. It was going to be a tough job stopping these two from wanting to be her parents! All the other impostors had hotfooted it out of Lizard Manor after their first visit, but the Greatbores seemed very determined. She was going to have to come up with something clever to get rid of them.

For the moment, though, she simply smiled and

said, "The best hotel in Pembrose is the Fishbone Inn."

To tell the truth, there was only one hotel in the village, and it only had one room. And it was horrible. You could eat there, too (fish only), but that wasn't a good idea unless you liked getting diarrhea.

"Try Timothy's fish stew," Minerva said in an angelic tone. "It's delicious!"

"Thank you, darling!" chirped Daphne. "We most definitely will! See you soon, my little Minerva!" She waved a white lace handkerchief out the window as the car creaked and screeched off down the hill.

Minerva just stared at them, frowning as they drove away. Anyone who knew her would have seen that she was already hatching a cunning plan.

Under the letter *M* in *The Universal Encyclopedia*, it said that Minerva was a warrior goddess. She had been born ready-made, complete with a shield and shining armor, after Jupiter had suffered a terrible headache. Minerva loved this story. She'd also been born ready-made, but inside a travel bag. Plus, the goddess's symbol was an owl, and Lizard Manor was full of them.

Maybe it was all just a coincidence. But Minerva had never felt so much like a warrior as she did right then. And as she waved goodbye to the Greatbores, she thought to herself, *You've got no idea what's in store for you! I'll be rid of you in no time!*

As she went back inside, the wind slammed the front door shut behind her, as if to underscore the terrible fate that awaited Arthur and Daphne.

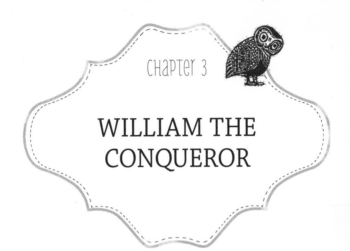

CHAPTER 3

WILLIAM THE CONQUEROR

Minerva thought things over as she ran upstairs. Portraits with worm-eaten frames covered the walls. With their green eyes, tiny ears, and snooty noses, their faces looked as old as the world itself. They stared at her grimly, their eyebrows raised in disapproval.

Minerva's eyebrows were raised, too, as she tried to come up with some plan to get rid of Arthur and Daphne.

Back in her bedroom, the water continued to *plip-plop* into the containers around the room, all of them now filled to the brim. Minerva took no notice and opened the old wardrobe that stank of mothballs. She scanned her clothes, unsure about what to wear. Nothing looked good. She closed the door and went to the room across the hall. She thought she remembered seeing something there that would be just right. She opened an old trunk and began rummaging through some beautiful dresses, shawls, gloves, and hats.

"There it is!" she cried, pulling out a dress that was a little short but warm enough. It was pleated and in a shade of green that would highlight her eyes.

Minerva hadn't bought a dress or a pair of shoes in her entire life. She'd found everything she needed in the closets and old trunks of the thirty-one bedrooms of Lizard Manor. There were lots of trunks in the attic, too — so many that Minerva still hadn't looked through all of them.

The clothes had all been packed carefully, with sheets of tissue paper between each piece so they wouldn't be ruined. They used to belong to the generations of people who'd lived in Lizard Manor. Minerva could find clothes for every size and every age. She loved trying them all on in different combinations.

Minerva put on the dress, her favorite rubber boots, and, for the finishing touch, a waterproof coat. She looked at herself in the big oval mirror near the door. Perfect. She was now ready for any weather.

"Oh, no!" she suddenly cried. "Something vital is missing!"

She went back to her room, reached under the pillow she never used, and pulled out her trusty slingshot. The goddess Minerva might have had a real sword, but slingshots were pretty good, too. She'd made it herself, using a stick she'd found in the garden and one of the strong rubber bands that Mrs. Flopps used to stop some particularly run-down window shutters from falling off. She'd become an expert markswoman, able to hit targets dozens of yards away.

Now Minerva was ready. She went down the stairs and headed for the back door. She was going into the village to buy a birthday cake for her party. But she'd have to be quick so she'd still have time for her homework. (Minerva didn't go to school in Pembrose, because Mrs. Flopps didn't trust public education. She taught Minerva herself.)

Minerva struggled to make her way across the potholed lawn. The wind seemed to want to blow her away. Mrs. Flopps was propped on a stool almost on the edge of the cliff, staring at a blank canvas. She was wearing a tartan cape that hung down to her feet and a hat that flopped down on one side of her head.

Mrs. Flopps was overweight, but Minerva didn't care. She loved her with all her heart. But what she loved the most about her was that Mrs. Flopps had never tried to take the place of her parents. The woman was as sure as Minerva was that one day they'd come back.

When she'd arrived in Cornwall, Mrs. Flopps had

been enchanted by the turquoise sea and the emerald green fields. No matter what the weather was like, she spent every day outdoors painting, only coming back inside for afternoon tea. She said that to make up for living the first half of her life in Talgarth Road, with all its horrible smells, she'd have to spend the second half breathing in the healthy sea air.

Minerva waved to her and shouted, "I'm going down to the village to buy a birthday cake!"

Mrs. Flopps replied with a shake of her paintbrush.

Minerva splashed across the lawn in her rubber boots. The house was surrounded by a huge garden, which was the kingdom of rabbits and moles. In spring and summer, it was covered by a carpet of orange and pink flowers. Then, in the evening, the flowers were replaced by dozens of fireflies.

All that was left of the front gate were two concrete columns crowned by two stone lizards. Even they had mostly crumbled, but you could still see their flicking tongues.

Minerva, still struggling against the wind, which really seemed to have it in for her, stopped for a moment. She was in a hurry, so why not take the shortcut to the village? It would be much faster, but . . .

That "but" was as big as the house. Minerva reached into her coat pocket. As soon as she touched her trusty slingshot, she felt much safer. She decided to risk it. Maybe in this bad weather, she wouldn't even need it. "Minerva Mint isn't afraid of anyone or anything!" She stuck her chin up, threw her chest out, and off she went.

She'd only gone a hundred yards or so when she heard a suspicious sound. A kind of *grrrrrr-grrrrrr.* She stopped and listened. The path wound its way through a grove. The sound had probably been nothing but the wind in the trees. She kept walking, now listening to every little sound.

There it was again: *grrrrrr-grrrrrr*!

"Trees don't growl," she said. Minerva looked around, her hand going back into her pocket and grabbing the slingshot.

Suddenly there was the sound of running feet.

"Pooh! I can't see a thing from here!" she snorted. Whatever it was, it was getting closer. She'd have to climb a tree. But that was no problem for Minerva, who'd been climbing trees more or less since she'd learned to walk.

In fact, she'd learned to do a lot of things at a very

early age. She could swim like a fish and sail a boat like a sailor. She could chop wood for the stoves and had a real gift for taking care of animals. She even knew how to tie a splint on a broken leg.

Since Minerva was so small and light, she scurried up a beech tree as nimbly as a squirrel and peered down. "Oh, no!" she exclaimed.

Her worst fears had come true: William the Conqueror was coming straight at her!

Hang on . . . she thought. *He's not after me. He's hunting something.*

William's latest prey turned out to be a big hare, which was running like lightning to escape. Coming up behind it and William was the equally evil Gilbert O'Sullivan. He was running at breakneck speed.

"I'm in big trouble!" Minerva gasped.

The problem with the shortcut was that it went right through the home turf of Gilbert's gang. If he saw her, she'd be done for. On the other hand, if she didn't try to save the hare, *it* would be done for. William the Conqueror never let his victims escape.

Gilbert O'Sullivan was the evilest kid in all of northern Cornwall. But he was also smart. He'd formed a gang with Damian Partridge and Lucas Dixon, and Minerva was right in the middle of their territory. In fact, their territory more or less ran right around Lizard Manor. So it was more or less impossible to avoid running into the gang, especially William the Conqueror, Gilbert's vicious dog. Minerva had been at war with them all for longer than she could remember!

She watched her enemies as she hid up among the leaves. The hare was fast, but William was relentless and he'd soon catch it.

Minerva took the slingshot out of her pocket along with an acorn. (She always carried a couple, just in case.) She looked around until she found what she was looking for: a nice big wasp nest hanging off a branch right in the dog's path! She took aim and hit it at just the right moment. The nest fell right on William the Conqueror's big, wobbly butt. He let out a howl and immediately turned tail to escape the cloud of angry wasps.

"Yes!" exclaimed Minerva as the hare disappeared into the undergrowth.

But Gilbert had seen it all. He was tall for eleven, with brown hair that was almost as curly as Minerva's. He put his hands on his hips and looked up at her. "I can see you, Minerva Mint!" he shouted angrily. "You're going to pay for this!"

Minerva didn't care. She looked out through the leaves and smiled. "Hi, Gilbert O'Sullivan! If I were you, I'd be more worried about my ugly dog. Those wasps looked really fast and really angry!"

Gilbert hesitated for a moment and then gazed in the direction in which William the Conqueror had disappeared.

Minerva took her chance. She dropped down to the ground and ran. By the time Gilbert had turned back around, she was a safe distance away. "You'll pay for this!" the boy threatened.

But poor William the Conqueror was now yelping pitifully in the distance. "Listen to that," cried Minerva. "Go and look after your dog. You're his owner. You don't want him to end up with a swollen butt!"

Gilbert might have been evil, but he loved William the Conqueror. He sped off in the direction of the yelping. "This doesn't end here, Minerva Mint!" he shouted over his shoulder with a dark look. "You're going to regret this!"

Minerva was sure of it, but she'd worry about that when it happened. For now, she had a birthday cake to buy!

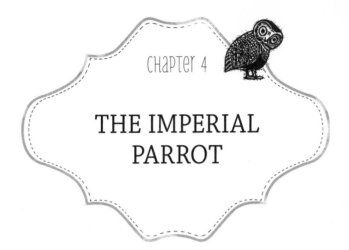

CHAPTER 4

THE IMPERIAL PARROT

The guidebooks described Pembrose as a "delightful little fishing village." It was nestled at the end of a cove between cliffs that towered over the sea. Its narrow streets, with granite cottages painted white, led down to the harbor, where there was a pebble beach strewn with fishing nets, ropes, and lobster pots. Fishing boats bobbed in the water, and a fish market was held on the quay.

The guides also said that Pembrose had been founded by smugglers. And the village was so well hidden, that could have been true.

In such a small place, everybody knew everybody else, as well as their business. Gossip was everyone's favorite hobby. But the villagers also enjoyed the fall and spring fairs, and the competitions for Village of the Year, the Most Beautiful Garden, the Best Cake, and the Biggest Cod.

Another thing the people loved to do was to tell stories about the Great Storm of 1927, the Big Freeze of 1964, the Great Blackout of 1987, and other milestones in the village.

The main street was called Plum Tree Avenue, and at that moment Minerva was charging along it. As she passed the Fishbone Inn, she saw the Greatbores' red car out front. There was a mountain of suitcases piled up in front of the door. Timothy, the kindly, bespectacled owner, was staring at them, shaking his head.

Minerva could hear Daphne's screeching voice from inside. "Arthur, hurry up with the suitcases! I can't wait to get into a hot bath and wash the smell of fox off me!"

Minerva just kept walking, a big grin on her face. The hotel didn't have hot water. She imagined how angry Daphne would be when she found out.

At the general store she bought a scrumptious-looking cake. It was a "ginger and papaya exotic delight." Minerva's mouth began watering the moment she saw it. It was so big, though, that when she carried the box, it was hard to see where she was going. Her rubber boots soon collided into a pair of patent leather shoes.

She put down the cake to see a blond girl with rosy cheeks and an expensive-looking raincoat over her school uniform. She was panting as if she'd been running.

"Stop her!" someone shouted from behind. "Stop, thief! Stop, thief!"

The girl dived behind a bush. But before disappearing, she held a finger up to her lips.

Just then, old Miss Lavender ran up, very out of breath. "Where is she?!" she yelled. "Where did that little thief get to?"

"She went that way," Minerva said, pointing in the wrong direction. "But she was fast. You'll never catch her."

"Oh, no! What will I do now?!" Miss Lavender moaned. "She took Napoleon!" The old woman waved a note in front of Minerva. "I found this in his cage. The kidnapper left it there!" she sobbed. "It's very threatening. But I've got to admit, it's beautifully written."

"What does it say?" asked Minerva.

"That I'll never see Napoleon again unless I promise to take him on a vacation to Brazil," sighed Miss Lavender. "But I don't want to go to Brazil! It's too far away! I want to stay in Pembrose!"

"Um," said Minerva. "Perhaps you could explain that to the . . . kidnapper. Maybe she'll understand."

"Poor me! Poor, poor me!"

Miss Lavender was a retired teacher who still tutored some of the local kids. Napoleon, her Brazilian parrot, was famous in the village for the rude things he'd say.

The old woman glanced nervously at Minerva. She was so upset that she hadn't even noticed that she was talking to the girl who lived up on the cliff. "Woe is me!" she continued to moan as she unhappily walked back home.

A moment later, a blond head appeared from behind the bush. "Is the coast clear?" it whispered.

"Yeah," confirmed Minerva.

The girl came out from behind the bush without a single hair out of place or mark on her coat. "Thank you," she said. "You saved my life. My name's Thomasina. What's yours?"

Minerva was delighted. She'd finally met the famous Thomasina Crowley! "My name's Minerva," she said excitedly.

Thomasina smiled. "Oh, that's who you are! Thank you for inviting me to your party!"

Minerva's face brightened. "Ravi's asked you already?"

"Yes! I've wanted to go inside Lizard Manor for ages! I've heard so many horrible things about that run-down . . . um . . . I mean . . . um. You know . . . er, excuse me."

"Oh, it really is run-down!" Minerva said.

They were suddenly interrupted by a terrible squawking. Thomasina opened her coat, and Napoleon poked his head out of an inside pocket. The parrot's feathers were ruffled and the bird looked annoyed. "Ugly old hag!" it said angrily. "Ugly old hag!"

"Why did you kidnap him?" Minerva asked, surprised to have found that Thomasina Crowley was actually a kidnapper.

"I didn't kidnap him. I set him free," Thomasina corrected her. "I've been planning this for ages. So, today, on my way home from school, I saw the cage on the windowsill and couldn't resist. I'll only take him back if Miss Lavender promises to take him to Brazil," she said firmly. An embarrassed expression suddenly crossed her face. "But . . . um . . . could you look after him in the meantime? I can't take him home. My parents wouldn't let me." Thomasina looked at Minerva with her big blue eyes.

Minerva didn't need to be asked twice. She looked after animals all the time, including rude parrots. "We've got plenty of room at Lizard Manor," she said.

"Thank you!" exclaimed Thomasina. "You're a real friend."

Minerva blushed. No one had ever said that to her before.

Thomasina gently picked up Napoleon and handed him to her.

"Old witch! Old witch!" the parrot squawked angrily. "Fish face!" Minerva placed him safely in her coat pocket.

"Thanks again," Thomasina said with a smile. "See you at four o'clock!" She then blew a kiss to Napoleon and ran off to the perfectly perfect Crowley Hall, her blond curls and red ribbon bouncing as she went.

Minerva gave Napoleon a scratch on the head to calm him down. She was quite sure that she was going to like having Thomasina as a friend.

CHAPTER 5

A CRESCENT MOON AND BLUE TIGERS

That afternoon, the wind grew even harsher. It was so strong that the people of Pembrose all stayed inside, afraid that a branch or roof tile might land on one's head. Only two solitary figures could be seen trudging along the narrow cobblestone streets. One was pushing a very squeaky bicycle.

Once they were out of the village, Ravi turned to Thomasina. "Hop on and I'll give you a lift," he offered shyly.

"Wow, what a gentleman!" exclaimed Thomasina. She climbed gracefully onto the seat, paying no attention to the fact that it was sopping wet from the rain. It would certainly muddy her beautiful clothes.

When she put her arms around him, Ravi turned as red as a tomato, but luckily she couldn't see his face. Ever since the first day at school, when Ravi had shared a desk with Thomasina, he'd had an enormous crush on her. She was beautiful. Perfect. An angel. She was ten but looked much older. And she knew many things.

Thomasina never paid much attention in class. Instead she secretly read books, never getting caught by the teacher. They were hidden in her desk. She chose books with interesting titles, like *Treasure Island* and *The Witches*. When Ravi had asked about them, she'd explained that they were adventure stories. And she'd used a tone of voice that made them sound like the most important things in the world. Thomasina absolutely loved adventure stories!

With a sigh, Ravi pedaled boldly into the blustering wind. He tried not to look at the sea, which grew farther and farther away beneath them. There was no way he was going to let Thomasina know that he was afraid of heights!

His mother had bought a big, stupid present to give Minerva, which he'd tied to his bike rack. He hoped it wouldn't fall off along the bumpy road.

For the umpteenth time, he told himself that he didn't like Cornwall at all. His name, Ravi, meant sun. It was the sun in India that he missed more than anything. He hadn't even seen the sun since he'd arrived here. But he imagined it as something pale and sad hanging in a gray sky.

They'd only come to his place with the miserable sun because of an ad on the Internet. It had said, "General store and post office for sale in Pembrose, Cornwall. Bargain price!" His mother had never been able to resist a bargain, so she bought it. And now here he was, riding up the driveway of the most lonely and weird house he'd seen in his life.

"We're here," he announced with a screech of his brakes.

Thomasina gracefully hopped off. She didn't have a single hair out of place, despite the furious wind. "Wow, what a place!" she exclaimed as she gazed at the enormous gray stone house. With its slate roof full of holes, ancient-looking walls, shutters falling off the windows, and crooked chimneys, it looked like a toothless old woman.

Ravi looked nervously at the roof as if he expected a flock of snowy owls to swoop him.

"Why didn't you tell me that it was such a cool house?" Thomasina asked excitedly.

"What?! You think it's cool?" Ravi said in surprise. He was still unable to take his eyes off the chimneys.

"Of course! It's even better than I thought! I wonder what it's like inside!"

"Yeah, it must be . . . um . . ." Ravi shivered. The last thing he wanted to do was see what it was like inside.

Minerva seemed to have a special radar to know when they'd arrived. The heavy front door had swung open the moment they'd stopped. She looked different without her hair up in her nightcap. Now her red curls stuck out in every direction like something gone crazy. On her right shoulder was a little parrot. Minerva ran to meet them. "You're here at last!" she cried excitedly.

The parrot, in a voice that was surprisingly loud for such a small creature, squawked, "Stupid idiot! Fish face! Stupid idiot!"

"Napoleon seems really happy here!" Thomasina said excitedly. "I knew that he'd be a new bird when I set him free!"

Ravi took the package off his bike and gave it to Minerva. "This is for you," he said, a little embarrassed. "It's a present . . . you know . . . for your birthday."

Minerva was delighted. "For me? Really?" she cried, grabbing the box.

Mrs. Flopps was the only person who'd ever given her birthday presents. (This year it was a painting of Lizard Manor.) But she wasn't as important as Ravi and Thomasina.

The boy was growing more embarrassed by the second. "It's . . . um . . . you know, nothing special," he mumbled. "It's just a sari. My mom said that you really liked hers."

"I've got a present for you, too!" Thomasina then announced, pulling a package out from her raincoat pocket. "Happy birthday!"

Minerva took the gifts and hugged them as if they were the most precious treasures in the world. "Thank you so much! Come inside!" she said, pointing to the door.

Ravi hesitated. There was something he'd wanted to ask Minerva since the first time he'd been there: "How come the house is called Lizard Manor?" He then looked around nervously before adding, "I don't like lizards very much."

"You're lucky, then!" Minerva smiled. "There are no lizards here at all!"

"So how come it's called Lizard Manor?"

"Who knows! This house is very mysterious," answered Minerva. "But come on! Everything's ready!" She was impatient to make a fuss over her new friends.

Thomasina rushed inside, while Ravi came last, dragging his feet. Just before he went inside, he saw a beautiful fishpond in the garden near the front door with a stone lizard on the edge. It looked as if it had been magically turned to stone while it had been lazing in the sun.

But he didn't have time to get a proper look before Minerva dragged him through the door. She closed it behind him with a crash that echoed through the house like a cannon blast. "Follow me!" she ordered.

Ravi immediately crashed into the huge suit of armor that was missing an arm and a leg. "I'm so sorry!" he said.

"Don't worry. It's really dark in here. The bulbs are all burnt out."

"Why don't you change them?" Ravi asked, rubbing his sore shoulder.

"Because they just burn out again," answered Minerva. "There must be something wrong with the wiring." She opened a drawer in a massive dresser and pulled out three candles and three cups. "We can use these." She lit the stubby candles off an oil lamp. Then she dripped a little wax into the cups to hold the candles and gave one each to Ravi and Thomasina. "This way," she said, pushing the two along in front of her.

No one could say that Minerva lives in a boring house, thought Ravi as he dodged the cobwebs full of huge spiders.

"My room's on the second floor," said Minerva, pointing to the stairs.

The three went up, making the stairs creak and groan as they went. Ravi looked up at the portraits staring back at him from the walls in the flickering light of the candles. "Wow!" he exclaimed. "Who are these creeps?"

"My ancestors," Minerva said.

"Oh . . . sorry. I . . ."

"No! You're right!" Minerva agreed. "They do look like creeps!"

Who knows if they really are my ancestors? she then thought. If only she could solve the mystery of who her parents were! Maybe her new friends could help her. She'd already decided to share the secret about the travel bag with them, and she was now dying to take them to her room. She could show them around the house some other time.

At the top of the stairs, though, a surprise was waiting for them: A chubby badger with a black and white face suddenly jumped out.

"What's that!?" cried Ravi in alarm.

"It's Hugo," Minerva said, bending down to scratch the creature on the head. Hugo had dug a huge network of tunnels under the house, which made it all the more likely that the house would collapse at any moment. The entrances were scattered everywhere. "He likes to surprise people," Minerva explained.

Napoleon, who apparently didn't like surprises one little bit, squawked, "Stupid idiot! Fatso!"

Hugo, who was apparently deeply offended, vanished into the darkness.

Minerva tried to calm the parrot down as she led them to her room.

Ravi was really impressed by the orange tent. Sitting in there with all the good things that Minerva had for them to eat (the exotic ginger and papaya cake and Mrs. Flopps's hot scones with homemade strawberry jelly) was very cozy.

They sat cross-legged in a circle, staring at the travel bag with its mysterious contents. They looked like members of some secret society. Their faces were glowing from the light of the oil lamp, and shadows danced all around them.

Minerva had put on the sari right away. It was emerald green and very beautiful. It made her look like a little Indian girl. Although it did look a little odd with her rubber boots, which she almost never took off. She sat with Thomasina's gift sitting in her lap: a compass. "Useful for adventurous expeditions," her new friend had said.

Minerva had just finished telling her story. She'd explained to them that every birthday she'd go through the things in the bag to try to figure out who she was and what had happened to her parents. "I figure that every year, I'm a little bit more intelligent," Minerva said with overwhelming logic. "So, there is a good chance that I might work out something new that I missed the year before."

As he swallowed his last mouthful of scone with jelly and fresh cream (the first thing he'd liked about Cornwall so far), Ravi thought that it all made perfect sense.

Thomasina stared at the big leather bag, covered with stickers from exotic places, with her sparkling eyes. "Wow! What an incredible story!" she cried. "What if you end up discovering that you're really a Watutsi princess . . . or a Polynesian queen . . . or the daughter of the Emperor of China?"

Minerva shivered with excitement. She'd thought the same sorts of things hundreds of times, but it was wonderful to hear them from someone else, too. It made it all seem more real.

"So, ladies and gentlemen," Thomasina finally said, "let's examine the evidence!" She also loved mystery stories — the ones with detectives who can work out everything about everyone. She sat up straight and put on her detective face. Holding an imaginary magnifying glass, she inspected the initials on the shiny brass buckle. "*MM*" she read. She turned to Minerva. "They're your initials. Minerva Mint. How's that possible?"

"Maybe Mrs. Flopps saw them and came up with a name that matched the initials," Ravi suggested. He thought that the most obvious solution was always the best.

"That's just what happened," confirmed Minerva. "But they still might be the initials of my mom or dad."

With her eyes half closed with concentration, Thomasina opened the buckle and the bag fell open. Holding their breath, they all leaned forward to look inside.

Thomasina reached in and pulled out a piece of paper that was a little yellowed with age. It was covered with tiny handwriting. There was a green wax seal on the top in the shape of a lizard. "What's that?" asked Ravi.

"The deed to the house," said Minerva. "The lawyer wrote my name on it," she said, pointing to a spot down at the bottom.

Ravi ran his fingers over the shiny wax lizard. It reminded him of the stone lizard on the edge of the fishpond. "You said there aren't any lizards in this house?" he asked Minerva.

"Not even one," she said firmly. Ravi became thoughtful.

Thomasina, who was feeling impatient, pulled out the big red book and turned it over in her hands. "*The Universal Encyclopedia*," she read. "How come there's only volume four?"

"No idea," said Minerva. "I looked for the other books in the library, but they're not there."

"Maybe they only published this one," Thomasina guessed.

"But they would have begun with the letter *A*!" Ravi objected. "Not *M*. That doesn't make sense."

"Things don't always have to make sense," Minerva said, with a shake of her red curls. "That's the beauty of it!" Ravi folded his arms as if he was defending himself against such nonsense.

Meanwhile, Thomasina had opened the book. There was a label glued onto the first page. It looked very old and had a picture of an owl with staring eyes. Underneath was written, "*Ex libris*." Then, in fancy handwriting, someone had written, "There's much more to this world than meets the eye. It all depends on how you look at it."

Thomasina frowned. "I wonder if your parents wrote that?" Then something else caught her attention. "Hang on, there's something else written here, too. 'Count the letters of Blue Tiger.'" She looked up. "What does that mean?"

Minerva was a little ashamed to admit that she

had no idea. She'd thought about it a million times, but all she could come up with was that there was no such thing as a blue tiger. She'd made very little progress over the last nine years.

Thomasina seemed to read her thoughts. "It must be some sort of riddle. We'll solve it together!" she said optimistically.

"Or maybe it means nothing at all," Ravi muttered so softly that the other two didn't hear.

Apart from the blue folder with the newspaper articles, the only other thing in the bag was the letter addressed to Mr. Septimus Hodge. "I've never found this Septimus Hodge," said Minerva. "The address is real, though. It's just that no one with that name lives in London and never has."

They examined the envelope like real detectives. It looked like a normal envelope — the kind you could buy anywhere. There was also a stamp with the Queen's head on it, only it had no postmark. The address was printed. Inside was a single sheet of paper on which was typed:

A crescent moon (in the kitchen)
Very ripe lightning-berries (count to five)
Three medium eggs (tap three times)
Two pints of molasses (turn to the right)
Milk (handle with care)
Mix (until your nose itches)
And finally, snail slime (and lots of it!)

All three sat in silence for a while, wondering what it meant. "They sound like instructions," Thomasina finally murmured.

"They're pretty weird instructions," said Ravi.

"It could be a recipe . . . for a cake maybe," Thomasina continued.

"With a crescent moon in it?" asked Ravi. "What sort of cake has a crescent moon in it?"

Thomasina was ready to argue. She wasn't used to people disagreeing with her. It never happened at Crowley Hall. Everyone did just what she said — the butler, the maids, even the grumpy gardener. "What do you know about recipes?" she sneered.

"I . . ." Ravi had nothing to say. He didn't know a thing about them. His mom did all the cooking at home. But he still wasn't going to give in. "Okay, if you're so smart, what are lightning-berries?" he asked. "I've never heard of them."

"Well, you're not from around here," Thomasina said, really starting to get annoyed.

"I've never heard of them either," Minerva interrupted. It wasn't easy to get a word in with these two bickering. "I thought it might be a recipe, too. I know all the berries and wild fruits that grow around here, but I've never found anything that could be a lightning-berry."

"See?" Ravi couldn't resist saying. "And she's lived here for nine years!" Thomasina just glared at him.

A fight would have broken out then and there if Hugo hadn't suddenly stuck his black and white face into the tent. The badger was curious about this odd gathering but was equally attracted by the smell of scones and jelly.

Napoleon, who'd been quite happy until then,

immediately puffed out his feathers. The parrot didn't like Hugo and wanted to make sure he knew it. "Lard butt! Lard butt!" he squawked from Minerva's shoulder. "Stupid idiot! Stupid idiot!"

Minerva tried to calm him down, but the parrot had only just begun. "Dum-dum! Lard butt! Poo pants!" he screeched.

Hugo figured that he wasn't welcome and vanished. Unfortunately, though, while they have perfect hearing and a wonderful sense of smell, badgers don't see very well. Hugo therefore didn't see that Mrs. Flopps was in his way.

The woman had left her afternoon tea to come see what all the commotion was about. And the second she put her foot on the top step, the little animal knocked her clean off her feet, sending her spinning through the air like a ballet dancer. She landed heavily on the stairs with a thump that seemed to make the whole house shake. "Augh!" she screamed.

Ravi, Minerva, and Thomasina rushed to the

scene of the disaster. They looked at Mrs. Flopps then at each other, trying not to laugh. The tension from a few moments before had vanished. But it was obvious that they were going to have to meet again later.

CHaPTer 6

MYSTERIES AT MIDNIGHT

That night, the wind grew even stronger. It howled through the village streets and slipped its icy fingers through window frames, down chimneys, and under doors. The moon was hidden behind a blanket of clouds, and the houses that still had lights on shone like tiny islands in the thick darkness.

Many people were still awake. They all felt strangely restless. But perhaps it was only the wind.

The Greatbores, though, had other reasons for being awake: they both had terrible stomachaches. "It must have been that fish stew," Daphne groaned.

She was propped up on two pillows on the uncomfortable bed.

"Or the cuttlefish stew," Arthur muttered, rubbing his stomach.

They were buried under a mountain of blankets. The room was cold, and they couldn't even take a hot bath. "I hate it here," complained Daphne. "Arthur, I want to go back to London. This place is not civilized."

"Come on, dear! Buck up!" whispered her husband, patting her hand. "Just a little patience."

"And I don't want to see another fox as long as I live. Or an owl."

"Come on, my dear," encouraged Arthur. He then sneezed loudly. He just knew he was coming down with a cold.

The church bell struck midnight. Most of the residents of Pembrose finally stopped their tossing and turning and fell asleep. Miss Lavender turned off her bedside light and wished Napoleon sweet dreams, wherever he was.

Peace descended on the perfect lawns of Crowley

Hall. But in the left tower, a light was still on — a small flickering light that cast shadows on the walls.

With his arms wrapped around William the Conqueror, Gilbert O'Sullivan was fast asleep on the top of the bunk he shared with his brother, Colin. Their cottage, which everyone called Blackbeard's Hideout, was silent, except for the snoring of the dog. He had been saved from the angry wasps just in the nick of time.

On the cliff top, Mrs. Flopps was snoring in living room number three. She'd fallen asleep in an arm-chair with a book about impressionist painters lying open on her big belly, which rose up and down as she breathed. Her bandaged leg was up on a stool. The foxes that were keeping her company were curled up on the couch.

Inside her orange tent and blissfully unaware of Gilbert and William the Conqueror's plans for revenge, Minerva was smiling in her sleep. She was dreaming that her parents were the Emperor of China and the Queen of the Amazon.

All of Lizard Manor's normal creaks and groans had stopped. The silence grew as thick as Jell-O. It was almost as if the furniture, paintings, and everything else in the house was as sound asleep as Minerva and Mrs. Flopps.

Standing lookout on the roof, only the owls were still awake. "*Woot-woot!*" cried Augustus, rolling his yellow eyes and twitching his feathery head. Then, as silent as a ghost, he took off into the dark sky.

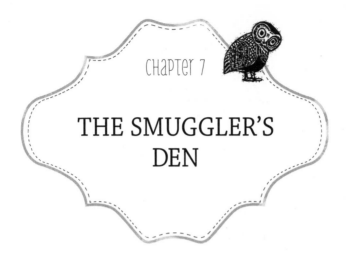

CHAPTER 7

THE SMUGGLER'S DEN

The next day was Saturday, so there was no school. The bells of the little stone church in the middle of the village were ringing out happily. The weather was still gloomy, but at least it wasn't raining.

Ravi was about to get on his bike when his mother came out from the store. She was wearing a sari as blue as the sky and was singing an Indian song.

She gently brushed back a lock of black hair from his forehead and handed him a bag. "I've made you some breakfast. There's something in there for your friends, too," she said with a wink.

"But I didn't tell you where I'm going!"

Mrs. Kapoor smiled. "I thought you were going to Lizard Manor."

The three friends had actually planned to meet at the old lighthouse under Admiral Rock on a spit of land that stretched out into the sea.

Ravi took the delicious-smelling bag and rode off at full speed. He messed up his hair again — he wanted to look his best for Thomasina. She really was kind of cute.

Meanwhile, Thomasina was still eating breakfast with her parents. But she was very distracted. It's not that there was anything wrong with the food — although Lady Annabella had complained to the maid that the tea was a little weak that morning, and Sir Archibald had said that he wanted the tea served in big cups. (He said that little ones were for sissies.) In the end, though, everything was fine. There were scrambled eggs, sausages, and perfectly crispy bacon. The toast was golden and the raspberry jelly was delicious.

Thomasina was wearing her Saturday dress with a pretty bow on the front (which made it hard to move) and polished shoes with straps. Sir Archibald and Lady Annabella were dressed from head to toe in tweed and were wearing riding boots. Both of them had rosy cheeks and hearty, strong bodies — possibly because of the huge breakfasts they ate every morning. They were surrounded by a pack of dogs, which were barking so much you could hardly hear a word anyone said. They spoke just the same, though.

Thomasina didn't bother to listen. All she could think about was *The Mystery of the Travel Bag*, a title she'd come up with herself. She couldn't have been happier. Finally she was having a real life adventure!

She took her napkin off her lap and placed it on the table. "May I be excused?" she asked. But no one could hear her over a golden setter that was barking furiously. Thomasina wasn't planning on waiting for an answer, anyway.

She ran to a hidden corner of the garden and,

when she was sure no one was looking, reached into the hedge and pulled out a stylish purse. Inside it she kept everything a girl could want for going on adventures. There was a compass, flashlight, burn cream, a map of Cornwall, and blocks of chocolate. She was ready.

Before meeting her friends, Minerva had to run an errand for Mrs. Flopps in the village. She stepped into the ladies' clothing shop opposite the general store, determined that she wouldn't get trapped in a conversation by the two owners.

"Minerva, what a lovely surprise!" exclaimed Araminta when she saw her. The younger of the two Bartholomew sisters was pretty and brunette.

"It's been such a long time since we saw you last!" said Gwendolyn, who was blond and taller than the Statue of Liberty. They were wearing identical outfits, which they'd designed and made themselves, and both had the habit of not letting their customers talk.

"Mrs. Flopps's tulle veil is ready," Araminta

chirped. She skipped behind the counter and pulled out a small box. She opened it to reveal a white veil that was so delicate it looked like a cloud. "Isn't it wonderful!" she said.

Just then, Minerva felt something wriggling in her coat pocket. *Oh, no!* she thought. *Not now!* She tried to calm the parrot down by stroking it, but it insisted on sticking its ruffled, feathery head out. "I've got to go!" she cried.

She grabbed the box and put the veil back in. "Thank you! It's beautiful!"

* * *

Ravi and Thomasina watched as Minerva rushed toward them. Her hair stuck out in every direction, as if it was trying to escape off her head. She had a small box under one arm, and Napoleon's head was sticking out from her coat pocket.

They were waiting for her outside the old lighthouse. It hadn't been used in years, and everyone in the village now called it the Smuggler's Den. It was right at the bottom of Admiral Rock. Minerva had chosen it for their meeting because that was where she went whenever she had to think about something important.

"Why did you bring him?" asked Ravi, pointing to Napoleon.

The parrot looked at him suspiciously and cried, "Stupid idiot! Lard butt!"

Minerva gave him a little pat. "He keeps getting into arguments with Hugo," she explained. "I thought he'd like to get out of the house for a while."

The boy and the parrot just stared at each other. "Dum-dum!" squawked Napoleon.

Ravi snorted. "I reckon you should take him back to his owner. Imagine how worried she must be."

Minerva immediately came to Napoleon's rescue. "No way! I'll only take him back when she promises to take him on a vacation to Brazil!"

"Whatever," said Ravi as they went into the light-house. "Hey, it's really dark in here!" he exclaimed in surprise. "Careful where you put your feet!"

"I'll take care of that," Thomasina said, pulling a flashlight from her purse.

Cobwebs hung thick from the ceiling like curtains. Small black things ran here and there in the gloom.

"Three centuries ago, this lighthouse was a famous smuggler's hideout," Minerva said as they climbed the spiral staircase.

"Yeah, and no one's cleaned it since then!" Ravi complained.

When they came back out into the sunlight in the lantern room, he breathed a sigh of relief. They went out onto the catwalk and sat down. It was great up there, watching the waves crash into the rocks as the seagulls circled high above the foam. There were also some puffins here and there drifting lazily on the current.

They divided up the breakfast Ravi had brought (three thick slices of banana walnut cake), while Minerva told the story of Daphne and Arthur. She also told them about all the other couples who'd come to Pembrose over the years, saying they were her parents just to claim the house.

"How can you be sure that they're not really your parents?" asked Ravi, swallowing the last piece of cake and wiping his hands on his jeans.

"Whenever anyone tells a lie, my feet tickle," Minerva said as if it was the most natural thing on earth. Ravi and Thomasina just stared at her open-mouthed. "And it's horrible! Like someone tickling my toes with a feather!" she explained. "Daphne and Arthur told so many lies that I could barely keep still!" Ravi and Thomasina just kept staring at her with an expression of disbelief. "Okay, let me prove it! Ravi, tell me three things. One has to be a lie."

Ravi thought for a second. "Okay. My best friend in India is named Anish," he began.

Nothing. Minerva's expression didn't change.

"I wear size seven shoes . . ."

Still nothing.

"My Uncle Darva is a postman . . ."

Minerva started grinning. She then jumped up and began hopping on one foot and then the other. She went red in the face and eventually doubled over with laughter. "He is not!" she cried through her tears.

Thomasina looked at Ravi. "Is he or isn't he?"

He shook his head. "No. Uncle Darva's a baker. He's really good, too."

Thomasina was now very excited. "That's incredible! Fantastic! Just think about how many things you could do with this power! You could expose all the liars in the world! You'd be a hero!"

Minerva wiped her tears and scratched her feet. "I'd rather not. I don't want anyone to know about it. I just need it to figure out if the people who say they're my parents are telling the truth. With everyone else, I just pretend not to notice. Everyone lies sometimes."

"So, Arthur and Daphne are lying?" asked Ravi. He was now ready to believe almost anything Minerva said.

"They tell lie after lie after lie," she said. "But they want the house. And since I can't prove they're lying, well, we've got to think up some plan to get rid of them!"

"*We've* got to?" asked Ravi in alarm. "You mean the three of us?"

Naturally, Thomasina was delighted. "What a great idea!" she cried, clapping her hands. She jumped to her feet and started walking around the catwalk. "So, what can we do to them? Put scorpions in their bed? Kidnap them? Hang them by ropes from the cliff until they promise to go away?"

Ravi was horrified. "Hey, calm down! You read too many adventure stories! The three of us need to give this some thought," he began. He suddenly realized that, in his anxiety to please Thomasina, he'd just committed himself to taking part in whatever crack-pot plan the two girls came up with.

"How much time do we have to get rid of them?" Thomasina asked Minerva.

"The lawyer will be here in a week," said Minerva. "If we could find my real parents before then, we'd have no problem!"

"Exactly," agreed Thomasina. "That way no one could ever try to take Lizard Manor away from you again. By the way, I've thought and thought about that strange letter in your bag. I think we have to follow the recipe," she said.

"Have you found any lightning-berries?" asked Minerva.

"Not yet," answered Thomasina. She gave Ravi a stern look. "But that doesn't mean they don't exist."

"Absolutely not," said Ravi.

Not sure if he was kidding or not, Thomasina just ignored him. "If we all work together, we'll figure it out. Can you come to Crowley Hall? We've got so many books in the library we're bound to find something."

Minerva was very excited. "Great idea! The books in Lizard Manor are hard to read because they fall apart as soon as you open them. Since the recipe was in my bag, it must be important for finding my parents."

Ravi couldn't keep quiet any longer. "How do you figure that? You think your parents will appear in a puff of smoke as soon as we mix it all together?" He then realized that what he said might have hurt Minerva's feelings, so he shut up.

"I've got no idea what will happen," Minerva admitted. "But I'm sure something will. Nothing is impossible!"

"Exactly!" cried Thomasina.

Ravi had been outvoted but he still tried to protest. "I think that —" He was interrupted by Napoleon.

The bird's tousled little head popped out from Minerva's pocket again. "Stop, thief!" he squawked. "Stop, thief! Stop, thief!" He seemed very upset about something.

"Pfft! What's wrong with him now?" snorted Ravi.

Minerva was immediately suspicious. "Something's not right here," she whispered, looking around.

"Stop, thief! Stop, thief!" repeated Napoleon.

Minerva, who was used to looking after herself, was better at sensing danger than the other two. She lay down and peered over the edge of the catwalk. "Oh, no!" she said, pulling her head back in immediately. She was so pale that her friends were worried.

"What's wrong?" asked Ravi.

"What did you see?" asked Thomasina.

"Shh!" Minerva said, putting a finger to her lips. "Maybe they haven't seen us. Stay down!"

"Who are you talking about?" Ravi insisted.

But just then there was a fierce growl and someone shouted, "Minerva Mint! Don't bother hiding, I saw you!"

"Oh, no!" she shrieked.

"And I saw your two friends!" shouted Gilbert.

They stood up and leaned over the lighthouse

railing. There were three of them down there, not counting William the Conqueror. They were surrounded by Gilbert's gang!

Gilbert smiled an evil smile. He was the tallest of the three. He stood there posing, with one foot on a rock and his hands on his hips. "I've come to settle a score! Like I promised!" he bellowed.

Minerva looked around. There was no one else around. They were trapped!

"Go away!" shouted Thomasina. She knew Gilbert and the other gang members. They went to her school, and the whole village knew about what they got up to.

"How come they've got it in for you?" asked Ravi.

"It's a long story," said Minerva. "We've got to get out of here," she said, moving toward the stairs.

"It's too late, Minerva Mint!" shouted Gilbert. "You'll never make it out of there in time." There was a note of triumph in his voice. He was like a cat playing with a mouse.

Minerva stopped. Gilbert was right.

"How dangerous are they?" asked Ravi.

"They think they own the village," said Minerva.

Someone kicked the lighthouse door open. It slammed against the wall, making Minerva, Thomasina, and Ravi jump with fright. They were coming!

"Can't we hide somewhere?" asked Thomasina.

"No. The only way out is that door and we can't go up any farther," said Minerva. "We can only go down . . ."

"And run right into them on those dark stairs!" Ravi sighed.

Minerva suddenly looked at him as if he'd said the most brilliant thing ever. She then looked at Napoleon's head sticking out of her pocket. "Wow!" she cried. "Ravi, you're a genius!"

"I'm a what?!" he asked with a puzzled expression.

Meanwhile, sounds of shouting and banging were coming from downstairs.

"Minerva, what are you going to do?" asked Ravi.

Thomasina was looking down the spiral staircase. "They're still at the bottom," she said. "They don't have a flashlight and it looks like they're having trouble finding their way in the dark."

"Good!" said Minerva. "Maybe my plan will work." She opened the box that the Bartholomew sisters had given her and pulled out the white veil.

Gilbert's gang made their way slowly up the stairs through the darkness. "Aren't there any lights in here?" asked Lucas. Damian bumped into him. "Hey, watch where you're going!"

"How can I watch where I'm going if I can't see any —" The words died on his lips. Something was moving about higher up the lighthouse.

"Hey, guys. W-what's that?" gasped Gilbert.

There was a supernatural light and a fluttering white . . . something! Whatever it was, it was terrifying and headed straight for them!

"Help!" cried Damian.

"A ghost!" screamed Lucas.

Then the something spoke to them in an inhuman voice: "Fish faces! Dum-dums!"

Damian was the first to run away, followed closely by Lucas. Gilbert tried to be brave, at least until the terrifying being started screeching, "Boogey monster! Boogey monster!" That was too much even for Gilbert, who shot down the stairs with William the Conqueror at his heels.

A minute later, Minerva whispered, "The coast is clear! You can turn off the flashlight, Thomasina."

The three children went down the stairs to get Napoleon. Minerva took the veil off him and put him carefully back in her pocket. "You're a hero, Napoleon!" she said.

"Ugly old hag!" he answered.

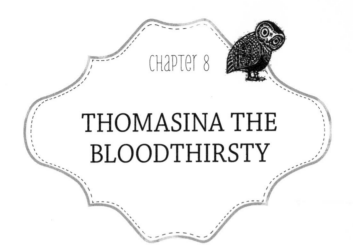

CHAPTER 8

THOMASINA THE BLOODTHIRSTY

The three friends had to wait a couple more days before they could meet again to find out what lightning-berries were. Thomasina's parents were convinced that idleness was the mother of all vices. So she had to practice her horseback riding, tennis, and fencing, as well as attend her piano lessons.

Minerva could have used this time to catch up with her homework. But with her desk sitting in front of a bay window that overlooked the garden, there was always something interesting to distract her. And then Napoleon, perched on her shoulder, made her jump all the time when he'd suddenly scream, "Old witch!" or "Stupid idiot!" every time an owl flew by the library window.

She was now certain that they were about to make some important discoveries about her parents. She also kept wondering what Ravi and Thomasina were up to. She was sure it was something more interesting than studying. In other words, she had far too much going on in her head to concentrate on any book. So, when the day finally arrived to meet her friends at Crowley Hall, it was an enormous relief.

She went downstairs wearing a beautiful dress. She didn't want to look out of place in Thomasina's perfect house. She'd tried to tame her wild hair and tie it with a ribbon. But her hair rebelled at any hint of being tied up, and she eventually gave in.

Minerva noticed a delicious smell. It was the season for jelly making and kitchen number three was full of big simmering pots. Mrs. Flopps was limping from one to the next, stirring the thick red liquid. She'd recovered from falling down the stairs but still needed to walk with a stick. "There's enough for at least a hundred jars this year!" she announced with a satisfied smile.

Mrs. Flopps sold her jelly and paintings of seascapes to the tourists who flocked to Cornwall during the summer. She actually made a small fortune so the two of them would have enough money to live throughout the year. But there wasn't enough left over to carry out the urgent repairs the house so badly needed.

"Mrs. Flopps, I'm going to Thomasina's," announced Minerva, walking into the kitchen.

The woman tasted the jelly to make sure it had enough sugar. "Mmm," she said with satisfaction. She had a big red stain right around her mouth. She licked her lips and said, "This is absolutely delicious!"

To get to Crowley Hall, Minerva had to go down to the village, but this time she kept well away from the shortcut. As she went by the Fishbone Inn, she narrowly missed Daphne and Arthur, who were out for a breath of fresh air.

Timothy was at the door of his pub, shaking his head as he watched them. When he saw Minerva, he was about to call out, but she stopped him just in time by putting a finger to her lips. He understood and gave her a wink instead.

Timothy may have been a disaster in the kitchen, but he was pretty smart. If he didn't wear Coke-bottle glasses and such old-fashioned clothes, and if he combed his hair once in a while, he might have even been quite good looking.

Minerva watched Arthur and Daphne staggering along the cobbled lane in silence. They still looked quite green after their fishy meals. *Excellent*, she thought. *They're ready for my cunning plan! Now all I have to do is think of one.*

When they were far enough away, she waved to Timothy and kept walking.

Across the street was the general store. The door was open, and she could hear happy music playing inside. Minerva saw Mrs. Kapoor dancing around the shelves. Someone pushed back the door curtain with tiny bells and Ravi appeared. His jet-black hair was combed back and looked hard.

"Hey, Ravi!" she cried. He seemed relieved to see her. He walked over to her with his hands in his jeans pockets.

"Tell the truth," Minerva said. "You're scared to go to Crowley Hall?"

"Nah, why do you think that?"

Minerva burst out laughing.

"Oh, sorry," said Ravi. "I forgot about the tickling. Okay, I'm terrified. Happy now? Thomasina always says how fussy her parents are. And that their gardener is a monster. I'm sure I'll accidentally stand on a flower, and he'll chase me with a pitchfork."

"Come on, don't worry! They won't eat us!"

Thomasina's parents actually turned out to be very kind and friendly. And, fortunately, the monster gardener wasn't there.

Crowley Hall looked more like a castle than a house. It was a huge building with towers and battlements. There was even a moat!

Sir Archibald and Lady Annabella welcomed their two guests like perfect hosts. They were dressed for fox hunting and their cheeks were redder than ever. They were surrounded by at least ten dogs that were barking all at once. "Minerva Mint?" Lady Annabella shouted to be heard over the din. "Of the Colchester Mints?"

"Of the Lizard Manor Mints," Minerva replied politely. She wasn't sure if she should curtsey or not. But she did anyway. Actually, she curtseyed so much that she almost fell right on top of the lady.

Although Lady Annabella was a little thrown by it all, she didn't let it show. "I see!" she screamed over the now hysterical dogs. "And you, young man?" she asked Ravi.

"I'm Ravi Kapoor of Mumbai," he answered in a faint voice.

"Ah! A *maharaja*, no doubt!" exclaimed Lady Annabella. Did she really think he was royalty?

Ravi muttered something unintelligible. Lady Annabella took it as a yes and smiled. "Well, my dear, next time you go back to India, please say hello to the Prince of Jaisalmer from me!" she said.

Ravi made a small gesture, which could have equally well meant yes or no.

Satisfied, the woman turned to her husband. "Come along, Archibald dear, the horses are ready."

"The hunt awaits!" answered the man, rubbing his hands together.

"Afternoon tea at five, please," Lady Annabella said to a maid.

"And please make sure it's strong enough!" Sir Archibald said. "I need a good strong cup of tea after hunting foxes! And some ham sandwiches."

The lord and lady of Crowley Hall then made their way slowly to the stables, their riding boots scrunching on the gravel drive.

Minerva was horrified. "They hunt foxes?!" she hissed to Thomasina. "We've got to stop them! We've got to do something! How about we cut their stirrups off? Then they wouldn't be able to get onto their horses."

Thomasina grinned. "Great idea!" she said, pulling out a pair of scissors from her purse. "I know a short-cut to get to the stables before them."

Minerva nudged Ravi, who was still dazed by being mistaken for a maharaja. "Come on, hurry up," she whispered. "We've got some work to do!"

* * *

After they'd sabotaged the fox hunt (at least for that day), Thomasina took her friends into the house as fast as possible so her parents wouldn't suspect anything.

Thomasina told them that Crowley Hall had lots of secret passages. "My ancestors needed them when one of them betrayed the king of England and had to run away during the night or get his head chopped off," she said, leading her friends through a series of rooms.

Once they got to the library, Thomasina went to one of the bookshelves. She gave one of the big books a push and a little door slowly opened between the shelves. "Come on, this way!" she said. "I'm the only one who knows about this passage. It goes to my hideout in one of the towers."

"Cool!" exclaimed Ravi, heading toward the door. It was so low, he had to bend down. Inside was a spiral staircase.

"After you," Thomasina said to Minerva.

When they had all gone through, Thomasina pushed a stone in the wall and the door closed silently behind them. "Ingenious, isn't it!" she said proudly. She took her flashlight out from her purse and led the way up the stairs. "It's really handy, too. At night, I can get all the books I want and then come up here to read them," she said pointing the flashlight up the stairs. "My parents don't like me staying up late, and they always check to make sure the light isn't on in my room."

As they went up, the stairs grew more and more narrow. It was hard to know where to put your feet in the dim light. Ravi tried not to think about how high up they were and clung to the wall as best he could.

At last they reached the top. Thomasina pushed open a wooden door and said, "Welcome to Thomasina the Bloodthirsty's hideout!"

"Wow!" cried Ravi.

Minerva was amazed. The tower was beautifully furnished with big, comfortable cushions scattered all over the thick carpet. A telescope pointed out a slit of a window from where you could see the coast. And there was a globe, lots of maps, and piles of books everywhere.

Thomasina explained that she kept all the things up there that her parents didn't approve of. There were books that weren't "appropriate" for a young lady, full of stories about bloodthirsty pirates and murderers. There was also a basket full of good things to eat, most of which were guaranteed to give you tooth decay.

Thomasina fell onto a cushion and asked, "So, what do you think?"

"It's wonderful!" said Minerva, collapsing beside her.

"Yeah. Not bad," Ravi muttered, sitting down opposite them.

Thomasina was happy that she'd impressed her new friends and immediately got down to business. "Unfortunately, I still haven't worked out what lightning-berries are. But I've brought some books up that might help us," she said, pointing to a pile of them on her right. "We should divide them up and check. Come on, let's get started!"

Lying back on the luxurious cushions, they started reading. Every now and then, just to keep their strength up, they'd grab some chocolate or one of the delicious cookies that the French cook had made. They didn't find any mention of lightning-berries, but they didn't give up.

It was far past teatime when Minerva suddenly cried out in excitement. She was holding a little book with the title *Oddities and Legends of Cornwall.* "I've found them!" she screamed.

Ravi, who'd almost fallen asleep reading his very boring book, mumbled, "Huh? What?"

"It even says what they look like," Minerva said.

"Show me!" Thomasina ordered. She clambered over to her side and read, *"Lightning-berry, also known as Kiss of Fire — A ruby red fruit with small, furry leaves. If not sufficiently mature, when touched it causes an allergic reaction that spreads to the entire body and burns like fire. It grows in the highest parts and most exposed cliffs of Cornwall, and is therefore difficult to pick. It is therefore extremely valuable."*

"We've done it!" cried Minerva. "Tomorrow we'll go looking for lightning-berries on the cliffs!"

Ravi immediately turned pale. On the cliffs? With his fear of heights?

"But it says the allergic reaction burns like fire!" he protested. There was no way he was going to mention his fear of heights.

"Simple. We'll pick the ripe ones," Minerva said.

Ravi wasn't about to give up so easily. "So how do we reach them? Are we going to go climbing up and down cliffs like Spider-Man?"

Minerva gave him a wink. "Things aren't always

easy. The harder something is, the more fun it is, don't you think?"

No. Ravi didn't think that at all. But Minerva did and so did Thomasina, and that meant that they were going lightning-berry picking tomorrow.

CHAPTER 9

OVER THE EDGE

That night, the rain poured down. The next day, there were huge puddles of water everywhere and it was freezing cold. Minerva decided to dress in layers, which she could take off if she got too hot climbing up and down the cliffs.

In the early afternoon, she came across Mrs. Flopps coming down the stairs. "Today I'm going out to study the nature of Cornwall," she announced. And it wasn't exactly a lie. Lightning-berries were certainly part of nature. They were a brand-new species of fruit that needed to be studied.

"Excellent!" said Mrs. Flopps approvingly, as she limped off to the kitchen to get back to her jelly.

Ravi was waiting for Minerva outside the general store. When he saw her, he smiled. He felt comfortable with Minerva now. But sparks still flew whenever he was with Thomasina — he still thought she was absolutely gorgeous!

Therefore Ravi's heart skipped a beat when they saw Thomasina outside the village. She looked stunning in her pretty dress and patent leather shoes. However, her shoes looked anything but comfortable. Minerva wondered how she was going to climb up any cliff with shoes like that. Apparently Thomasina had a habit of dressing up no matter what she was doing.

Thomasina pulled a map out from her fashionable purse and looked at it. "We've got to climb to the top of Traitor Rock," she announced, pointing to a spot on the map. "It's the highest and most inaccessible point around here. We'll definitely find lightning-berries there!"

Ravi gulped but said nothing. He was afraid his voice would shake. He followed the two girls, dragging his feet like a condemned man on the way to the gallows.

* * *

The ground was terribly slippery, and it took a long time to follow the trail that led to the top of Traitor Rock. When they arrived, they were all sweaty and out of breath, except for Thomasina. She casually took a pair of binoculars out from her purse and began searching the rocks for lightning-berries.

Minerva gazed out at the turquoise sea, which had never looked so huge or so full of the promise of voyages to faraway places. From up there they had a breathtaking view of the bays, rugged cliffs, and granite headlands buffeted by the wind and foaming waves. Minerva felt the salt on her skin and the wind blowing through her hair as if it was trying to pull it off.

"Aha!" said Thomasina as she spotted something

below them. "I see something red. It's got to be lightning-berries!"

"How can you be so sure?" asked Ravi, who felt
faint at the thought of what awaited him.

"Well, I'm not really. The only way to be sure is to
climb down and see!"

Ravi looked over the rocky edge. "Look, there's

no way I'm going *tooo*—" He suddenly disappeared. A sudden gust of wind had literally blown him off his feet and right over the edge.

Minerva and Thomasina were paralyzed with shock. But then they heard a faint cry: "Help!" They crept cautiously toward the edge, clutching hard onto the short tufts of grass that covered the hill.

Two heads, one blond and one red, poked out over the edge and looked straight into Ravi's terrified eyes. He'd only fallen a short distance and was now lying belly-down against the sloping cliff. "I can't climb up," he moaned. "Everything's covered in moss. It's too slippery."

"Leave it to me!" cried Thomasina, reaching out her hand to him. "Come on, grab on!" she urged him.

"I can't reach you!" cried Ravi.

But Thomasina had leaned too far forward and suddenly slid down the cliff as well. She went right past Ravi, grabbing hold of him as she went. Luckily, though, a narrow ledge stopped their fall. It was even harder to climb back up from there. At least, that's what Minerva thought as she gazed down, wondering what on earth she could do to save them.

This was the first time that Ravi had been in any real danger in his life. And even though he was afraid of everything, he suddenly felt calm, cool, and collected. Fear of heights or no fear of heights, he had to do something. "Put your foot in my hands!" he ordered Thomasina.

She didn't understand. "Why would I do that?"

"Just do as I say! Put your foot in my hands and then climb onto my shoulders. That way you'll be able to climb back up."

"Okay, but what about you?" she asked.

"Just do as I tell you!" ordered Ravi in a voice that meant he wasn't going to argue.

Taken by surprise by this new Ravi, Thomasina obeyed without question. He was quite tall, so, after climbing up onto his shoulders, Minerva was able to drag her back up. Minerva gave her such a hug that they ended up falling onto the grass, belly up. It was Thomasina's turn to be sweaty and out of breath. "Now what?" she asked.

They went back to look over the edge. But at that precise moment, the narrow ledge, which had been supporting the combined weight of Ravi and Thomasina, broke off the cliff face. Minerva and Thomasina closed their eyes as hard as they could.

"Hey, look. I'm still here!" came a faint voice. The two girls opened their eyes again and breathed a sigh of relief. Ravi was now clinging to a tuft of grass that stuck out from among the moss and rocks.

Minerva's voice was now shaking. "How long can you hold on? Can you stay there until we get someone to help you?"

"Um . . . that depends. How long will you be?"

"To get to the village and back will take at least forty minutes."

"I can't hang on here for forty minutes!" Ravi already felt his grip giving way. "Maybe I can hold on for five minutes. There isn't a stick or something up there you can drag me up with?"

Minerva and Thomasina looked around. All there was on the cliff top was grass and tiny yellow flowers.

"There's nothing here," Minerva shouted, poking her head back over the edge.

Ravi tried to stay calm so he wouldn't frighten her. "Well, maybe I'm done for," he said with a small but brave smile.

Minerva's face disappeared again. A minute went by with no sign of either girl. Ravi couldn't hear anything except the wind whistling in his ears.

Maybe they've gone to get help? he thought. *Maybe*

they saw someone. Someone with a stick. Please hurry.

For all that time, Ravi had avoided looking down. He knew that if he did, he'd be finished. But his hand was aching so much that it wouldn't be long until he'd have to let go. And then . . .

"Can you hang on for another minute or so?" Minerva suddenly cried, her freckled little face framed by a tangle of red hair peeking back over the edge. She smiled encouragingly. "We've got an idea."

Ravi felt a little better. "Okay, but hurry!" He prayed the clump of grass wouldn't give way. What was this idea they'd come up with? And why was it taking them so long?

At last, he saw something snaking its way down the cliff toward him. It looked like a rope. Where could they have gotten a rope from?! Without thinking, Ravi grabbed it with one hand and then the other, and pulled himself up.

When he got to the top he was very surprised to find the girls shivering in their underwear!

Minerva was a genius! She'd suddenly started tearing off her clothes and told Thomasina to do the same. Then, using the scissors that Thomasina kept in her purse, they'd cut their clothes into strips and tied them together.

Thomasina, who was the tallest and strongest, had then tied one end around her waist. She'd then laid down on the ground with Minerva on top of her, hoping their combined weight would be enough to support Ravi.

After getting over his embarrassment of seeing them like that, Ravi smiled the biggest smile that Minerva had ever seen. He slowly reached into his pocket, pulled something out, and held it toward them. His palm was badly grazed, but sitting in the middle of it were five shiny red berries!

"No way!" Minerva and Thomasina cried at once.

Ravi's smile grew even wider. "While I was climbing up, I saw them right in front of me, so I grabbed them!" he said. "They must be ripe since I can't feel anything. No burning." He looked at his friends with the proud expression of a returning hero.

Thomasina couldn't resist. "Ravi, you're fantastic!" she screamed, throwing her arms around him and making him blush as red as a tomato.

CHapter 10

SNAIL SLIME

That night, two shadows could be seen moving quietly toward Lizard Manor. The moon was a tiny crescent. The wind caressed the grass, and on the chimneys, three owls stood lookout. Their yellow eyes glowed in the darkness.

The biggest of the two shadows made a signal: two long whistles and a short one. Just like they'd agreed. The front door immediately opened a few inches, and a curly head popped out.

"Come in!" Minerva whispered. "Everything's ready."

She led the way with a candle. The house was quiet, and there was a strong smell of strawberry jelly in the air. "Mrs. Flopps has just gone to bed," Minerva whispered. "Did you have any trouble getting out?"

"None at all. I'm an expert at nighttime escapes," Thomasina said proudly. She was wearing a cape as dark as the night with a hood that hid her blond curls.

"I told my mom that I was having a sleepover at your place," said Ravi. "She's happy we're friends." Ravi still didn't think that the recipe would help Minerva find her parents. But after everything that had happened that afternoon, he was starting to think that even the impossible might happen. Anyway, they had to get to the bottom of this once and for all.

They slipped quietly along the hallway. Minerva whispered, "I got some molasses, milk, and eggs."

"And I brought a snail," Thomasina said, pulling a small box out from her purse. "I saved it from Angus McAllister, who wants to kill them. He says they ruin his roses!"

Everything was ready in kitchen number three. There was a large bowl on the table. Thomasina read the recipe. "There's a crescent moon shining through the kitchen window. Perfect."

"And here are the five lightning-berries," said Ravi, dropping them into the bowl.

"Three eggs," Minerva said. She tapped them three times against the edge of the bowl, trying to follow the recipe to the letter. She dropped the egg yolks and whites over the red berries. She then added two pints of molasses while turning the jar to the right. Then, very carefully, she added some milk.

She then started stirring it all with a wooden spoon. After a little while, her nose started itching ever so slightly, just like the recipe said. But maybe that was just the smell of jelly that still hung in the air.

At any rate, Thomasina then very gently placed the snail on the wooden table. It started moving straightaway, leaving a lovely trail of slime behind it. "Instant snail slime!" she cried.

They added it to the mixture and then just stared

at it, not knowing what to expect. Maybe Minerva's parents really would appear in a puff of smoke, just like Ravi had said.

But nothing happened.

They stared and stared at the bowl, willing something to happen, but nothing did. "Let's wait a bit longer," suggested Ravi. "Just to be sure." But he was as disappointed as the others.

They had to face facts: Nothing was going to suddenly appear out of that sticky mess. It didn't even look good to eat — with or without the snail slime.

Minerva tried to stay optimistic. "Well, we tried. Maybe we didn't follow the recipe properly or . . ."

"Maybe." Ravi picked up the recipe and read it through a few more times, frowning. "Do you have a pencil?" he asked Thomasina. She took one out of her purse and handed it to him. He drew a series of arrows on the paper to link the information in parentheses. When he'd finished, he exclaimed, "Wow! They form a message!" He showed it to his friends. "Look!"

They all read it together, *"In the kitchen, turn to the right, count to five, tap three times, until your nose itches. Handle with care, and lots of it!"*

Ravi looked around. "We're already in the kitchen. . . ." Just then he noticed a row of large red tiles that went right around the room about three feet above the floor. He walked out the door then came back in again, stopping in the doorway. He counted five tiles to the right and tapped three times on the fifth one. But nothing happened. His nose certainly wasn't itchy. "I was wrong," he muttered.

Then Minerva had an idea. "Maybe this isn't the right kitchen! Let's try number two!" They rushed down the hallway, not caring how much noise they made.

Kitchen number two was still filled with smoke from the stove. Ravi followed the instructions again. But again nothing happened. "Let's try number one!" Minerva whispered.

Kitchen number one was flooded because of a broken pipe. There was a terrible stink of mold in there, and the floor was under two inches of water. Ravi tapped three times on the fifth tile to the right. This sent a small cloud of dust into the air, which made his nose itch. He sneezed. "Hey! It sounds hollow!" he cried. He tried moving the tile and eventually pulled it clean off the wall. Behind it was a small hole. Without hesitation, he stuck his hand inside. "There's something in here!" He pulled out a small wooden box.

His friends immediately rushed over to him. Minerva held up the candle to see better. It was small and made of dark wood. And it was very old. On the top was a picture of a round tower with some words:

"*Ordo Noctuae*," Minerva read. She looked at the others. In the flickering candle light, they looked as confused as she did. "What does that mean?"

"No idea," said Thomasina. "Come on, Ravi, open it!" she urged. "I'm dying to see what's inside!"

"You open it, Minerva," Ravi said, handing her the box. "This is your mystery," he whispered with an encouraging smile.

Minerva took the box in her shaking hands. She slowly lifted the lid. Inside was what looked like a tiny flute. She picked it up and held it in the palm of her hand. All three just stared at it. There didn't seem to be anything special about it at all. Minerva turned it over in her hands, then, driven by some irresistible impulse, lifted it to her lips and blew.

She was no musician. She had played on the grand piano in Lizard Manor and soon discovered that she had no ear for music at all. But playing this little flute came naturally to her. She started playing a beautiful melody that surprised them all. Immediately, there was a flutter of wings outside the window. Minerva stopped playing, and everyone just listened as the flapping became louder and louder.

They ran out into the garden to see what was going on. All three were stunned: the sky was full of owls. White and majestic, they were flying this way and that on their huge wings. They seemed magical.

"There must be at least a hundred of them!" cried Ravi in amazement. "What's going on?"

Minerva looked at the little flute she still held in her hand and smiled. She'd just come up with a brilliant plan to get rid of Daphne and Arthur.

CHAPTER 11

THE ATTACK OF THE OWLS

The next day, the sun came out big and bright. Even Ravi, as he was riding to school on his bike, had to admit that it was just as beautiful as the sun in India. It made the grass shine emerald green and lit up the thousands of yellow and pink flowers. The sea glittered turquoise and crystal clear. As Ravi rode, he whistled a tune. A gentle breeze that smelled of salt and spring blew over his face. He sped up and shot like an arrow down the path through the meadows. After everything that had happened, he felt full of energy. He felt . . . well, he felt like a hero in one of

Thomasina's adventure stories! He smiled when a grazing sheep took fright at him darting by. Ravi decided that Cornwall wasn't so bad after all.

The people in the village were happy to finally see the sun again. They all went out into the streets of Pembrose to chat with neighbors and just enjoy the lovely weather.

Daphne and Arthur were almost back to their normal color after fasting and refusing all the food that Timothy offered them. And, like everyone else, they felt so happy to see the beautiful sun that they decided to take a stroll. "Come along, my dear," said Arthur lovingly as he helped his wife along. "The lawyer will be here soon. We'll take possession of the house, tear it down, and build dozens of vacation villas to rent to tourists at ridiculous prices!"

"And we'll get rid of all those foxes!" Daphne mumbled. Her stomach still did not feel quite right. "And we'll ship that Minerva off to boarding school!"

But she was forced to stop her daydreams when Minerva herself suddenly appeared in front of them.

"Oh . . . hello, my dear!" exclaimed the woman, trying to smile.

Minerva seemed very concerned about the health of her, er, parents. "You look terrible!" she said with pretend concern.

"We've certainly felt better," Daphne muttered.

"Maybe you're seasick," Minerva suggested.

"But we haven't been on a boat, my dear," Arthur pointed out.

"The food here is disgusting," Daphne snorted, forgetting to smile for a moment.

"I'm sorry," Minerva mumbled. "Everyone here just loves Timothy's cooking."

"Maybe it was just a little heavy for us city folks," Arthur said, trying to make Minerva happy. "Too much garlic, possibly. We're not used to garlic."

"But we're much better now, darling," Daphne piped up.

"That's good!" exclaimed Minerva. "So, we could have a party to celebrate you coming back! We could have it at Lizard Manor. With all the foxes and

Hugo — he's my badger. And we can have music. I just learned to play the flute. Listen to this." She pulled the little box out from her pocket, took out the flute, and began to play.

Immediately, dozens upon dozens of owls swooped down from every direction and began circling over their heads, getting closer and closer. And closer and closer. And even closer and closer.

Daphne immediately screamed in terror and, without waiting for her husband, ran to their red car, started the engine, and drove off.

Arthur, after recovering from his astonishment, hotfooted it after her. "Stop, darling! Please wait for me! I want to go, too! Please don't leave me here!"

But she didn't stop. She just went faster and faster down the narrow street, which became more and more narrow, until she scraped all the paint off one side of the car. Arthur just kept running after her, screaming, "Daaaarling! Don't leave me here!"

Minerva stopped playing and put her little flute back in its box. A smile spread across her face. She was very happy. Her plan had worked to perfection. The owls had broken down Arthur's and Daphne's last defenses.

One by one, the majestic birds flew away until there wasn't a single owl left in the sky.

"Extraordinary!" commented Dr. Gerald, who'd watched the whole amazing spectacle unfold along with a group of stunned villagers. "I've never seen so many owls in my life. I wonder what brought them here."

"Maybe they're migrating," suggested an old lady loaded down with shopping bags.

"It's probably to do with climate change," said an old fisherman thoughtfully.

"Hmm," said the doctor. "I don't believe that owls are migratory." But then he noticed the little box in Minerva's hand and read the writing on the top, "*Ordo Noctuae.* That's Latin." Dr. Gerald knew a lot of things and was very smart. In fact, everyone in the village came to him if they had a problem to be solved.

"What does it mean?" asked Minerva.

"Well, a rough translation would be, 'Order of the Owls.' *Noctua* is the Latin word for owl. It's a way of describing the magic of the night," he said with a wink.

The doctor then walked off to his office. Outside the door, there was already a line of perfectly healthy, elderly patients who, more than anything else, wanted a sympathetic ear to listen to their complaints and gossip. And maybe Orazia, his nurse, would make them all a nice cup of tea.

* * *

The sunset that evening was spectacular, filling the sea and sky with broad brushstrokes of red and orange. A few boats bobbed gently in the distance. The coastline with its high granite cliffs was wrapped in a golden glow, while the seagulls floating in the air currents cried for sheer joy.

Thomasina, Ravi, and Minerva were enjoying the spectacle from the catwalk of the lighthouse. Minerva had told her friends everything about the way the owls had swooped down, sending Daphne running for her life. Three times, actually. Ravi and Thomasina

never tired of hearing it. Minerva's plan had worked perfectly!

"I wish I'd been there!" Ravi chuckled.

"I had to do something. Timothy's food had weakened their defenses, and they were ready for the final blow," explained Minerva. "But I didn't want you there, too, since it would only have made them suspicious."

Thomasina ran her finger over the box. "So, the writing means 'Order of the Owls'." Her eyes suddenly lit up. Ravi, who'd seen that light several times over the last few days, was worried. They lit up like that when she was planning some adventure. "Hey, guys!" she said, "Why don't we form a secret society, a club of our own, and call it the Order of the Owls?"

"The Order of the Owls," repeated Minerva. "I love it!"

But Thomasina still had that light shining in her eyes, "You do realize that we've already completed two missions!"

"Two?" asked Ravi, puzzled.

"Well, we got rid of Arthur and Daphne, and Miss Lavender has decided to take Napoleon on a vacation to Brazil. My mom told me today."

Minerva couldn't have been happier. "*Yesss!* An overseas trip will do her a world of good, too. She always seems so sad and lonely."

"And Napoleon will learn new words. They might even be polite ones!" said Ravi. All three burst out laughing.

Ravi had to admit that he really liked Thomasina's idea. After all, he'd done pretty well up on the cliff. He'd even managed to get over his fear of heights. Well, almost.

"Actually, we've solved two and a half cases," he said. "We also solved some of the mystery of the letter to Septimus Hodge."

Minerva put her hand to her throat and touched the chain from where she'd hung the tiny flute. She'd decided to always keep it with her because she was sure that it belonged to her parents.

"If the flute was so well hidden, it must be important," said Ravi.

"And it's definitely a clue for finding Minerva's mom and dad," said Thomasina.

"We know that it can be used to call owls," Minerva said. "Maybe they could lead me to my parents."

"Or maybe the flute does something else as well," suggested Ravi. "I reckon we'll find out more about it once we've solved the other mysteries. Like who Septimus Hodge is and what all the other clues in the bag mean, like the note in the encyclopedia."

"Count the letters of Blue Tiger," Minerva recited from memory.

"It's like a puzzle," said Ravi.

Minerva smiled. They had so many things to do together that it meant she'd be spending a lot more time with her new friends, Ravi and Thomasina. It meant they wouldn't leave her. "We should start now!" she said enthusiastically.

"First we've got to make a club rule," objected

Thomasina, who was much more experienced with secret clubs than the other two from all the books she'd read. "And a password." She sighed. "We are the defenders of Pembrose! We punish the wicked and help the weak!"

"Speaking of the wicked," Minerva said, "next time Gilbert and his gang plan something, we'll have the owls on our side. I wonder how they'll react to being swooped by owls!"

"Absolutely!" Thomasina said. "I can hardly wait!" She then thought for a moment. "But we're going to have to find another hideout. They know about the lighthouse."

"We need a top-secret headquarters," Minerva agreed.

"We'll have lots of adventures!" cried Thomasina. "This is going to be great!" she said, putting her arms around the shoulders of the other two.

Ravi instantly turned as red as a tomato, but he still said, "Our first mission has to be to find Minerva's parents, though, okay?"

Minerva thought it was perfect. Everything was perfect. The sunset. The hug. Her new friends. "The Order of the Owls is going to have some great adventures!" she shouted at the sea and sky, now both as red as fire. "You'll see!"

Elisa at age 3

As a child, I had red hair. It was so red that it led to several nicknames, the prettiest of which was Carrot. With my red hair, I wanted to be Pippi Longstocking for two reasons. The first reason was that I wanted to have the strength to lift a horse and show him to everyone! The second was that every night my mother read Astrid Lindgren's books to me until she nearly lost her voice (or until I graciously allowed her to go to bed). As I fell asleep each night, I hoped to wake up at Villa Villacolle. Instead, I found myself in Milan. What a great disappointment!

After all of Lindgren's books were read and reread, my mother, with the excuse that I was grown up, refused to continue to read them again. So I began to tell stories myself. They were serialized stories, each more and more intricate than the one before and chock-full of interesting characters. Pity then, the next morning, when I would always forget everything.

Elisa today

At that point I had no choice; I started to read myself. I still remember the book that I chose: a giant-sized edition of the Brothers Grimm fairy tales with a blue cloth cover.

Today my hair is less red, but reading is still my favorite pastime. Pity it is not a profession because it would perfect for me!

GABO LEON BERNSTEIN

I was born in Buenos Aires, Argentina, and have had to overcome many obstacles to become an illustrator.

"You cannot draw there," my mom said to me, pointing to the wall that was smeared.

"You cannot draw there," the teacher said to me, pointing to the school book that was messed.

"Draw where you want to . . . but you were supposed to hand over the pictures last week," my publishers say to me, pointing to the calendar.

Currently I illustrate children's books, and I'm interested in video games and animation projects. The more I try to learn to play the violin, the more I am convinced that illustrating is my life and my passion. My cat and the neighbors rejoice in it.

Gabo

WHAT'S NEXT FOR
THE ORDER OF THE OWLS?

An overpowering archaeologist visits Pembrose to see Merlin's cave. Is it possible that it's the sorcerer's cave, or is it just a legend to attract tourists? Minerva and her friends will solve the mystery!

The ghost of a fierce pirate is scaring everyone in Pembrose. Was the late Black Bart so mean that his spirit cannot find peace? Minerva and friends will find out!

FIND OUT MORE ABOUT MINERVA MINT AND HER FRIENDS AT WWW.CAPSTONEKIDS.COM